PUNK ROCKER
from HELL

Sue Gough

illustrated by Kate Barry

Contents

Chapter One

It's my hair and it's not fair

Mum and I had another row last week. We've been having rows ever since I turned thirteen, and that was months ago.

Some of our rows are about clothes. But most of our rows are about my hair. That's what this row was about. I wanted to get a punk haircut. Mum said "no". I said it wasn't fair. I was thirteen, old enough to make up my own mind. And after all, it was *my* hair.

Mum still said "no".

I think adults are a pain about things like hair and clothes. They like saying "no". It gives them a feeling of power.

They like to have a moan, too. Our hair and clothes give them something to moan about. They get together with their friends and whinge. They say things like, "I don't know what the world is coming to", or "What *do* they think they look like?" (I can tell you what *they* look like. They look *boring*, like black-and-white photos.)

When adults say "no", they don't have to give you a good reason. They say dumb things like, "What will our friends say?" If you try to argue, they get heavy. They say things like, "You think you are going out looking like that? Over my dead body!"

Sometimes, if you keep on and on and on, you can talk them round. Adults seem to get tired before kids do, and when they get tired they give in. I was trying this with Mum.

I tried all the things that have worked
before, such as:

"All the other boys in my class have punk
haircuts."

"You are ruining my life."

"You do not treat me like a real person."

It was in the morning, before school, so Mum wasn't feeling tired. I couldn't talk her round.

I said, "But *why*? Give me one *good* reason why I can't have a punk haircut."

"Because you'll look silly," Mum said.

"But it's my hair," I said.

"But I have to look at it," Mum said.

"You don't have to look at it," I said.

"Of course I have to look at it," Mum said. "What do you expect me to do? Close my eyes every time you come into the room?"

I said, "It's not fair. You can do what you want with your hair."

Mum started to get a bit aggro. "I bet you would whinge if I made myself look silly," she said.

"No I wouldn't," I said. "Anyway, you don't want to do anything with your hair. You like to look boring."

I shouldn't have said that. Mum said "Hmmm . . . ," and a funny look came over her face.

Chapter Two

The thing in the kitchen

I decided to have another go at Mum when I got home from school. She would be tired by then.

That afternoon I came home and walked into the kitchen. I saw ... I saw ... It's not easy to talk about this ... I saw this thing in the kitchen. It looked like a punk rocker from hell!

This thing had a head that was shaved on one side. The hair on the other side was not shaved. It was striped red and green. It stuck out all spiky, like a toilet brush.

The face was enough to frighten Freddie right off Elm Street. It was dead white. There were black rings around the eyes and it had black lipstick. I took one look at its weirdo earrings and then I took another look. They were not earrings. They were safety pins.

The punk rocker was wearing a black T-shirt with rips in it. There was writing on the T-shirt. It said "Metallica". The punk turned around and I could see that there was writing on the back of the T-shirt, too. It said "Megadeath" and "Skate to hell". I could see that this was a head-banging punk.

You should have seen what else the punk was wearing! It had shiny, stretchy tights under the T-shirt. The tights were striped like tiger skin, all yellow, brown and black. I looked down. The punk was wearing Doc Martens boots. All in all, it was not a pretty sight.

Then the punk rocker from hell spoke to me. It said, "Hi, Jason. How was school?"

I couldn't believe it. That was my mum's voice. This was the worst moment of my life. I said "Aaaaaaargh!"

She ran her fingers through her spiky hair
and spoke again.

She said, "What's wrong with *you*?"

I didn't say a word. I was in shock.

"Cat got your tongue?" she asked.

I tried to talk but all that came out was a kind of squeak. Mum, the punk rocker from hell, started to laugh.

"I thought I'd have a bit of a change," she said. "I don't want to be boring any more. What do you think? Do you like it?"

"You look, you look, you look ... *silly*," I said.

"Well, you don't have to look at me," Mum said.

"I can't help looking," I said.

"I'll get out of your way then," she said.

Mum picked up her purse and headed for the door.

"You're not going out looking like that, are you?" I asked.

"We need some milk," she said.

"I'll go," I said. "You can't go out looking like that. One of my friends might see you."

"So what?" said Mum, tossing her awful spiky hair. "You said you wouldn't whinge if I made myself look silly."

Mum headed for the door. I ran past her. I got between Mum and the door.

"Don't you go out there, Mum," I said.

"Don't be silly Jason," she said. "I'm only going to get some milk."

"Over my dead body," I said.

"Ooooooh," said Mum. "You do sound upset."

I grabbed the purse out of her hand and ran out to get the milk.

Chapter Three

Hot and sweaty

Phew! At least no-one would see her *this*
time. But what was I going to do about
tomorrow? If she went out, people would
see her and everyone would start to talk. I
hate it when people talk about your mum.
There are some kids at school with weirdo
mums and other kids are always teasing
them. A lot of fights start about things like
that. I don't like fighting. I'm kind of small
for my age. If I had long, spiky hair I might
look a bit taller.

I started to worry about something else. What was Dad going to do when he came home and saw her? He would freak out! Then I began to feel better. I was sure that Dad would talk her round so she wouldn't go out of the house until she looked normal again. I didn't know what she could do about the shaved bit of her head. Perhaps she could wear a wig for a bit.

I bought the milk at the corner store and started to head home. That's when I ran into more trouble. My friends Brett and Zac had spotted me.

"Hi dude," said Zac. "We were just on our way to your place. I've got to pick up that video I lent you. It's due back tonight."

"Oh, no," I thought. "I've got to stop them from coming over to my place." I tried to think fast.

"I'll go and get it," I said. "No need for you to come all the way home with me. I'll run home and grab the video and run back and give it to you."

Brett and Zac looked at me and then looked at each other. Their faces had a look on them that said "Huh?"

"Hey dude, what's up?" asked Brett. "It's cool. We were coming over anyway. Remember you said I could have a go at your Nintendo?"

It was a bad scene and it was getting worse. We got to my place and my mind was working at mega-speed. Perhaps I could still stop them from seeing Mum. Perhaps I could get them straight to my room without her hearing us.

"Shhhhh!" I said. "We've got to be quiet. Mum's got the flu and she's having a rest."

"What?" asked Zac.

Brett started to tell him for me. "Jason said his mum ..."

Mum heard us. She called out from the kitchen.

"Is that Brett and Zac? Hi guys. Want a soft drink?"

I nearly died. I had to stop Brett and Zac from going into the kitchen.

"She shouldn't be up," I said. "She's got a fever. If you go near her you'll catch it. I'll get the drinks."

Brett and Zac looked at me and then at each other. Just like before, their faces had a look on them that said "Huh?"

They went upstairs. I went and got the
drinks. Then we sat around in my room,
talking. Brett had a go at my Nintendo game
and I gave Zac back his video, but they
didn't go. They were happy just hanging out.
It seemed like they were going to stay
forever. I tried to talk as if everything was
cool but I was feeling hot and sweaty . . . and
scared!

I was trying to work out how to get rid of them, when there was a knock on the door and I heard Mum's voice.

"Got some chokkie bikkies for you guys," she said.

I ran to the door like greased lightning and opened it just a tiny bit.

"Thanks Mum," I said. "I can't let you in right now. It might put Brett off the Nintendo. Just leave the bikkies on the floor outside and I'll pick them up later."

"Jason, you are *weird*," said Mum. I heard her walk away.

Brett and Zac looked at one another as if they agreed.

Zac looked at me. He could see that something was wrong.

"Hey dude, you look all hot and sweaty. Looks like you're coming down with the same thing your mum's got."

It was the perfect excuse.

"Yeah, I think you're right," I said. "You dudes had better go. I don't want to give it to you."

"We'll go and say goodbye to your mum," Brett said.

"Oh no," I thought. "This is it. THE END."

Just then the phone rang and Mum answered it. Talk about "saved by the bell".

"Don't worry. She's on the phone," I told them. "I'll tell her goodbye for you."

I heard them go out of the front door and I said "Phew!"

Chapter Four

Sucked in, Dewdrops

Five minutes later I heard Dad's car arrive. I heard him come in and go into the kitchen. I waited for all hell to break loose. It didn't. What was going on? I went downstairs towards the kitchen. I could hear Mum and Dad talking as if everything was normal. I crept up the hall and put my head around the kitchen door.

Was I going crazy or something? The punk rocker from hell had disappeared. There was Mum looking like her boring old self. Even her hair was back to normal. I began to shake. If Mum was not the punk rocker, then who was the weirdo I had seen in our kitchen? Perhaps it was an alien who went around stealing other people's voices. Perhaps it was still here, hiding in one of the cupboards.

Then I saw something on the kitchen table. It was kind of rubbery, with red and green hair sticking out of it. Mum saw me. She picked up the rubbery thing and tossed it at me.

"Here, catch," she said. I caught it. It was a punk rocker wig.

"Ever been had?" she said. Dad was laughing his head off.

"Sucked in, Dewdrops," he said.

I tried to look cool.

"I knew all the time," I told them, but I could see they weren't going to believe that one.

"The wig is for you, anyway," Mum said. "It's trick or treat night tomorrow and I thought you'd like it."

I put it on and looked in the mirror. It looked *wicked*. I began to feel better. Perhaps I could live without a real punk haircut for another week.